MW00896538

Published in 2020, by Coco Publications

Coldwater, OH 45828

Brite-Hamel, Allisten

If Mommy's Being Honest

Story by Allisten Brite-Hamel / Illustrations by Jana Bloom

ISBN
978-1-5323-8770-8

Library of Congress Control Number
2020909297

Book Design by Kelly Grantham

PRINTED IN THE UNITED STATES OF AMERICA

Dedications

Lord, I thank you for your never-ending mercy, love, and understanding. By your saving grace, there is always hope.

David and Dawson, there are no words, but only feelings to describe how much I cherish and adore you. All that you are is all that I'll ever need.

Mom, Dad and Connor, thank you. I love and appreciate you more than you know.

This book is dedicated to all of those who struggle with mental health issues. Know you are never alone and that through each season, in growth or despair, God is always with you.

Allie Hamel

My dear, sweet baby

If Mommy's being honest,
raising you is no easy task.
Thinking of you is my priority,
selfish days all in the past.

You are my fairytale,
my life's wide-awake dream.
Handcrafted in the Heavens,
God stitched you seam by seam.

More beautiful than ever,
you are my angel child,
filled with sweet moments –
some scary, some wild.

The greatest blessing you are,
but with no manual you came.

They sent us home a new family;
our lives would never be the same.

Our first weeks were oh-so scary,
and some nights felt more than long.
But so precious were you,
God's gift, my soul's new song.

If Mommy's being honest,
you came with growing pains,

but like flowers in the spring time,
so much beauty came from rain.

Mommy's been reborn herself,
for this is all brand new.
So bear with me while I am learning;
I might cry sometimes, too.

I'm trying my best every day –
I'm giving you my all.
Know it's never my intention
when we both stumble and fall.

This new path we have is curvy,
full of changes and God's plan.
We both must trust He'll get us through
when we don't think we can.

You changed my world, sweet little one,
gave me hardships filled with purpose;
so many moments filled with peace
but also pain beneath the surface.

Full of fear and racing worry,
days could be hard to get through.

But as you were growing and sprouting,
I was blooming, too.

If Mommy's being honest,
I won't always get it right.
There'll be days yet to come
where I'll be the one up through the night.

Never alone, though often lonely,
Motherhood seldom makes any sense.
But atop each hill and through each valley,
our love remains constant and immense.

Our time will pass so quickly;
Mommy wants to hold on and make it last.
All these moments in the present,
too soon will be the past.

These stages come in waves of grace;
like the tides, we ebb and flow.
For it's when I look upon your face
that hope is all I know.

I'd give my life, my dreams, my breath,
anything that I could do,
and I'd do it all again each day
for just a moment loving you.

Love always,
mama

What is a Perinatal Mood Disorder?

Perinatal Mood Disorders (PMDs) consist of: Baby Blues, Postpartum Depression, Postpartum Anxiety/OCD, Postpartum PTSD and Postpartum Psychosis. Each can be characterized as a mother being in distress for various reasons with unique symptoms. Postpartum Depression is the most common diagnosis and used to be used as a blanket statement to cover these unique disorders. As more information has been brought to light, doctors are seeing the importance of a correct diagnosis and that each woman struggles differently. It is also important to recognize that PMDs are not only a postpartum issue. Roughly 15% of women report experiencing severe depression or anxiety during pregnancy. One in six women will struggle with a PMD, as it is one of the most common medical conditions for women during and after pregnancy.

Baby Blues vs. Perinatal Mood Disorders
Baby Blues is believed to be experienced by most mothers, affecting up to 80% of women in the first two weeks postpartum. Symptoms include impatience, irritability, fatigue, crying for no reason, moodiness, restlessness and difficulty transitioning into new life with a baby. It is very normal for new mothers to feel most, if not all, of these symptoms the first few weeks after baby arrives. It is not normal, however, to experience feelings of hopelessness, or for these symptoms to persist or worsen. When concerning symptoms last longer, intensify, or begin after two weeks postpartum, the mother is at risk of going undiagnosed with a serious and sometimes life-threatening perinatal mood disorder.

Postpartum Psychosis
Postpartum Psychosis is the most severe type of PMDs and it is very rare, affecting .1% of mothers. Early intervention is crucial. Unlike the other disorders, it is likely that the sufferer is completely out of touch with reality. In fact, the most serious symptoms to look for are paranoia, hallucinations, rapid mood swings, a decreased need for sleep and strange newfound religious beliefs. Postpartum psychosis is an emergency situation and should be taken very seriously. The onset is typically noted shortly after birth or within the first two weeks after delivery. It is temporary and very treatable with professional help.

Signs & Symptoms

Emotional
- Feelings of being overwhelmed, hopelessness, emptiness, or sadness
- Crying often or for no reason
- Irrational fears about potential harm that could come to the baby
- Feelings of overwhelming anxiety, irritability, or rage
- Persistent doubt in the ability to be a mother
- Thoughts of running away
- Feelings of losing it, going crazy, or having no control of yourself
- Intrusive thoughts of harming yourself or the baby
- Feelings of indifference about life and death
- Inability to relax
- Lack of motivation and inability to finish normal daily tasks
- Extreme guilt for not being okay
- Constant, racing, obsessive thoughts
- Constantly checking on the baby
- Separation anxiety
- Having trouble bonding/forming an emotional connection with baby

Behavioral
- Inability to sleep when the baby does
- Avoiding leaving the house
- Afraid to be alone or take care of the baby
- Panic attacks
- Loss of interest in things you once enjoyed (anhedonia)
- Excessive sleeping or getting too little sleep
- Poor hygiene: not showering or brushing teeth when needed
- No sex drive
- Unable to focus
- Chronic exhaustion or hyperactivity
- Distrust of anyone other than you watching the baby

Physical
- Insomnia
- Physical aches and pains
- Loss of appetite
- Headaches

Resources

postpartumdepression.com
This site not only has information and videos regarding postpartum depression, but it also has a printable plan that families can use to help prepare for the postpartum period. Many doctors and mothers put much care and thought into the pregnancy and birth plan, but fail to be prepared for the months after baby arrives. This is a great tool for all expecting mothers to support everyone in the family and not just the new baby.

postpartum.org
Toll-Free 1-855-255-7999 | Texting 604-255-7999
This site offers support services and information for your whole family. There are resources available not only for mothers, but fathers as well, who can also struggle with perinatal mood disorders. They have contacts all across the US and Canada. Their numbers for contact also include a texting line for those who may struggle with phone anxiety.

National Suicide Prevention Lifeline:
Toll-Free 1-800-273-8255 | Crisis Text Line 741-741
If you are experiencing suicidal thoughts or feel you are at risk of harming yourself or your baby, please reach out — there is always hope. This lifeline provides completely free and confidential support for those in distress. They are open 24 hours a day, seven days a week, for anyone of any age — including non-English speakers.

postpartum.net
This site is packed full with knowledge and resources regarding perinatal mood disorders but is especially beneficial if you or someone you know is experiencing postpartum psychosis. This site has an online coordinator listed who can help aid families and women while they navigate going through this hardship. It is important to note this service should be used to learn more and seek help in non-emergency situations. Postpartum psychosis is an emergency and help should be contacted immediately if it is suspected.

Supporting a Mom with a PMD

1. Empathize with and believe her
2. Know the symptoms and research what she is going through
3. Help her get rest and uninterrupted sleep
4. Help her establish her village; a community of women raising her up in action and prayer
5. Gently encourage her to get help (make phone calls/arrangements if needed)
6. Remind her to eat, drink, and get fresh air as often as she can
7. Respect her boundaries and what makes her uncomfortable
8. Acknowledge when she has made progress, but be okay with where she is at
9. Make her freezer meals or send some gift cards for nights she is too exhausted to cook
10. Include her and invite her to things even if she will most likely say no. She may say, "Yes!"
11. Help her find joy in new things if she has lost it in her old hobbies
12. Don't compare her to others or yourself and help her do the same
13. Tell her she's doing a great job and that you see how hard she is trying
14. Remind her she is not a burden and that she is very needed in your life
15. See if there is anything she could use help with around the house
16. Remind her this is only a season of life and that feelings are not permanent
17. Try not to say things like, "it all goes so fast" and, "don't blink." These can be overwhelming statements
18. Don't tell her to enjoy every second; it's impossible
19. Tell her she is loved, appreciated, and has a purpose here
20. Tell her to pray and cry out to the Lord, He is who will sustain her

Bible Verses

Jesus wept.
John 11: 35

The verse above makes up the shortest sentence in the entire Bible. Let this reality humble you; Jesus wept. This means the Lord of Lords, King of Kings, the One Who numbered the stars, knows how it feels to cry. In His humanness, Jesus allowed what breaks our hearts to shatter His. He allowed our failures and devastations to crush Him. Never, for a single second, doubt that the Lord doesn't understand your every struggle.
Through His death and Resurrection, Christ has made your tears sanctifying; by His cross, He made your struggles Holy. Rest in the truth that you are never alone in this life.

To the overwhelmed Mama:
Matthew 11: 28-30; Psalm 40: 1-4; 1 Peter 5: 6-11
To the anxious Mama:
Jeremiah 29: 11; Matthew 6: 34; Deuteronomy 31: 6
To the Mama who feels like she's losing it:
2 Timothy 1:7; Philippians 4: 5-9; 1 Peter 4: 12-13; Psalm 94: 18-19
To the Mama doubting her call to Motherhood:
Ephesians 2: 10; Proverbs 31: 25-31; Philippians 1:6; Romans 8: 28-30
To the Mama who needs hope:
Psalm 61: 2-5; Romans 8: 38-39 & Romans 5: 3-5; John 16: 33
To the Mama who feels unknown:
Psalm 139

Friend, I leave you with this: Motherhood is not swallowing you. Just as all the previous seasons in your life have come and gone, this too shall pass. As the sleepless nights seem endless and your body grows weary, ponder these verses and breathe in the truth that Christ Jesus knows and is with you. There is not a second through the day where the Lord, your God, is not holding you and your child in the palm of His mighty hand. The joys and agonies of your heart are heard. Each day, from now until the end of time, has already been planned. Rest easy in His presence, breath in the new life He has gifted you, and embrace the overwhelming joy that He is always offering. The best is truly yet to come.

About the Author

Allie Hamel is wife to her high school sweetheart, David Hamel, and mother to their son, Dawson. She is a stay-at-home mom who, after struggling with debilitating postpartum anxiety and depression, has felt called to bring about awareness and understanding for those who struggle with perinatal mood disorders. It would bring her great joy if this book helped just one person, but she dreams this message can spread far and wide, reaching multiple generations of women and helping them and their families for years to come.

About the Illustrator

Jana Bloom began her career as a graphic illustrator, and is now in her 14th year teaching art to children in grades kindergarten through eighth grade. She is grateful for the opportunity to work with her former student, Allie, on this meaningful project.

CPSIA information can be obtained
at www.ICGtesting.com
Printed in the USA
LVHW072209081020
668359LV00008B/364